BIG MEAN MIKE 🐾

For Spencer
M. K.

For my fuzzy and
dear friends at
Candlewick Press
S. M.

First edition 2012

Library of Congress Cataloging-in-Publication
Data is available.
Library of Congress Catalog Card Number 2011046623
ISBN 978-0-7636-4990-6

12 13 14 15 16 17 TLF 10 9 8 7 6 5 4 3 2 1

Printed in Dongguan, Guangdong, China

This book was typeset in Matrix.
The illustrations were done digitally.

Candlewick Press
99 Dover Street
Somerville, Massachusetts 02144

visit us at www.candlewick.com

BIG MEAN MIKE was the biggest, toughest dog in the whole neighborhood. He had a big, mean bark. And big, sharp teeth. He wore a big black collar with gleaming silver spikes, and his claws were big and mean and very, very pointy.

Best of all, he had a big, mean car that he liked to drive around the big, mean streets. It made a big, mean sound whenever he revved the engine.

"Here comes Big Mean Mike!" the other dogs would say. "He's the biggest, toughest dog in the whole neighborhood!"

Everyone knew how big and tough he was, and that was just the way Mike liked it.

One Tuesday, Mike decided to buy a new pair of combat boots.
He liked the way they made his feet look extra big and mean.

He came out of the store and admired his big, shiny car.
Then he opened up the big, wide trunk.

And there, next to the big, tough spare tire, was a tiny, fuzzy bunny.
"Hey!" said Mike. "How'd you get in there?"
The tiny, fuzzy bunny blinked up at him sleepily. It was *very* cute.

Mike picked up the bunny and quickly set it down on the sidewalk. Big, mean dogs and tiny, cute bunnies did *not* go together.

He peeled out and sped away, revving his engine a few extra times for good measure.

On Wednesday, Mike got in his car to drive to the gym. He opened up the glove compartment to get out his gym pass. But when he reached inside for the shiny plastic card, he felt something else instead.

Something . . . soft.

Something . . . cuddly.

He leaned over to peer inside.

The tiny, fuzzy bunny was back. And this time, it had brought a friend.

"Hey! I told you to get out!" Mike barked at the first bunny.
He pointed at the second bunny. "That goes for you, too."

Mike scooped up both bunnies, hoping that no one was looking.
He put them down outside the car.

He felt their little eyes watching him as he drove away.

On Thursday, there were three tiny, fuzzy bunnies sitting on the hood.

"Get off my car, you bunnies!" Mike shouted.
"What if someone sees you up there?"
The bunnies did not get off. They looked at him and wiggled their cute little noses.

Mike picked them up one by one and put them on the ground.
Then he spelled it out for them.
"Big, tough dogs do not hang around with tiny, fuzzy bunnies, okay?
So beat it. Scram. And don't come back!"
Mike found excuses not to use his car for the next few days.

WORKINGDOG'S
COOPERATIVE
BANK

The next weekend, Mike had a ticket to the Monster Truck Show. He had been looking forward to it for months. Monster trucks were big and mean—just like him! The show was in the next town over. Too far to walk. Mike went out to his car. He looked carefully under the hood.

He checked the trunk.

Then he peeked inside
the glove compartment.
"Heh," said Mike. "Nothing to
worry about after all."

When he got to the stadium, the parking lot was full of big, mean dogs getting out of their own big, mean cars. None of them were as big and mean as Mike, of course, but some came pretty close.

Mike turned off the ignition. The keys slipped from his grasp and landed on the floor. A pair of tiny white paws reached out from under the seat and picked them up.

"ARRGH!" cried Mike. He stared in dismay as four tiny, fuzzy bunnies hopped up onto the seat. They twitched their soft bunny ears and blinked their cute little eyes.

"No more bunnies!" Mike yelled.

"Get out of my car!"

The bunnies just sat there, looking at him.

"Fine," Mike growled. "Stay in there. I'm not missing the show because of you!"

He snatched up his keys and slammed the door. The bunnies gazed up at him with their sweet little fuzzy faces.

"Gosh, you guys are cute," Mike said. Then he looked around. "I mean, I hate cute! Grrr! I'm Big Mean Mike!"

He started to walk away. Then he stopped and looked around again.
A parking lot full of big, mean dogs was not a very good place for little
bunnies. He couldn't leave them there alone. It wouldn't be safe.
"Arrgh!" Mike growled. He had no choice.

"All right, bunnies," he said. "You can come with me. But I don't want
the other dogs to see you." He got his gym bag out of the trunk. "Hop in
here, and be quick about it." The bunnies hopped into the bag.

Mike hurried inside and found his seat. The Monster Truck Show was just starting. It was AWESOME.

Mike felt his gym bag moving on the seat beside him. The bunnies were sticking their little heads out, peering around with bright, excited eyes. "All right," Mike whispered. "You can watch. Just try not to let anyone see you."

One by one, the bunnies climbed out onto Mike's lap. They nibbled pieces of his popcorn. They bounced in excitement whenever a big, mean truck cleared a jump or a little car got crunched under big, tough tires.

Mike couldn't bring himself to make them go back in the bag. They were having such a good time! And so was he. It was kind of fun to have someone to watch the show with. Even better to have several someones. Even if they *were* tiny, fuzzy bunnies.

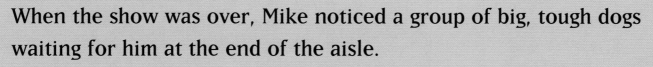

When the show was over, Mike noticed a group of big, tough dogs waiting for him at the end of the aisle.

"Got some new little friends there, Mike?" one dog asked.

"Didn't figure you for the cute and cuddly type," said another.

"Guess you're not so big and mean after all!" a third dog barked.

Soon all the dogs were laughing and pointing. Mike didn't know what to do. This was terrible! His image was ruined!

HERE, KITTY, KITTY

Then one of the bunnies leaned forward and made a tiny growly sound. The other bunnies all joined in. Mike looked down at them.

Grrrr...

Slowly, he smiled a big, mean smile. Then he looked back at the other dogs. "You know what?" Mike told them. "I don't care what you think. I'm Big Mean Mike! I can hang out with whoever I want! I like these bunnies. They know how to have a good time. And they're adorable! Any of you got a problem with that?"

The other dogs all took a step back.
"No problem here!" the first dog said.
"Yeah, we were just kidding around," said the second dog.
"Good," said Mike. "Now, get out of our way. My friends and I
are going home."

From that day on, Big Mean Mike went back to driving around the big, mean streets in his big, mean car. He still did everything in his own big, mean way. And everywhere he went, four tiny, fuzzy bunnies went with him.

And that was just the way Mike liked it.